BY THE TIME THIS YOU READ

Written by Jennifer Lanthier
Illustrated by Patricia Storms

BEWARE: Alien Insect!

Published in Canada by Clockwise Press Inc., 56 Aurora Heights Dr., Aurora, ON Canada L4G 2W7

www.clockwisepress.com

solange@clockwisepress.com   christie@clockwisepress.com

10 9 8 7 6 5 4 3 2 1

Library and Archives Canada Cataloguing in Publication

Lanthier, Jennifer, author

By the time you read this... / by Jennifer Lanthier ; illustrations

by Patricia Storms.

ISBN 978-1-988347-05-9 (hardcover)

I. Storms, Patricia, illustrator II. Title.

PS8623.A69877B92 2017   jC813'.6   C2016-908093-5

Design by CommTech Unlimited
Cover illustration by Patricia Storms
Printed in China

The text in this book is set in GelPenUpright.

By the Time You Read This...

By Jennifer Lanthier

Illustrations by Patricia Storms

CLOCKWISE
PRESS

To James Lanthier & Kelci Gershon. By the time you read this, I'll have thought of a better dedication. – J.L.

As always, for my Guido. By the time you read this, I will love you even more. – P.S.

...our **Scientific Experiment of Glorious Doom** will be terminated.

KABOOM!

By the time you read this, our **Epic Battle of Giant Robots Versus Alien Insects** will be over.

Armageddon.

By the time you read this,
our **Magical Zoo of Mystical Creatures** will be closed.

Liberated.

By the time you read this,
our **Neverending Novel of
Awesome Adventures**
will be finished.

The End.

By the time you read this,
our **Precarious Portal for Intrepid Explorers**

will be sealed.

10 9 8 7

9

8

7

Access Denied.

By the time you read this,
our **Time Travel Tower
of Ultimate Power**
will be enemy territory.

...I will have forgotten why we were ever friends.

Yours UNtruly,

Your EX-friend,

Oscar

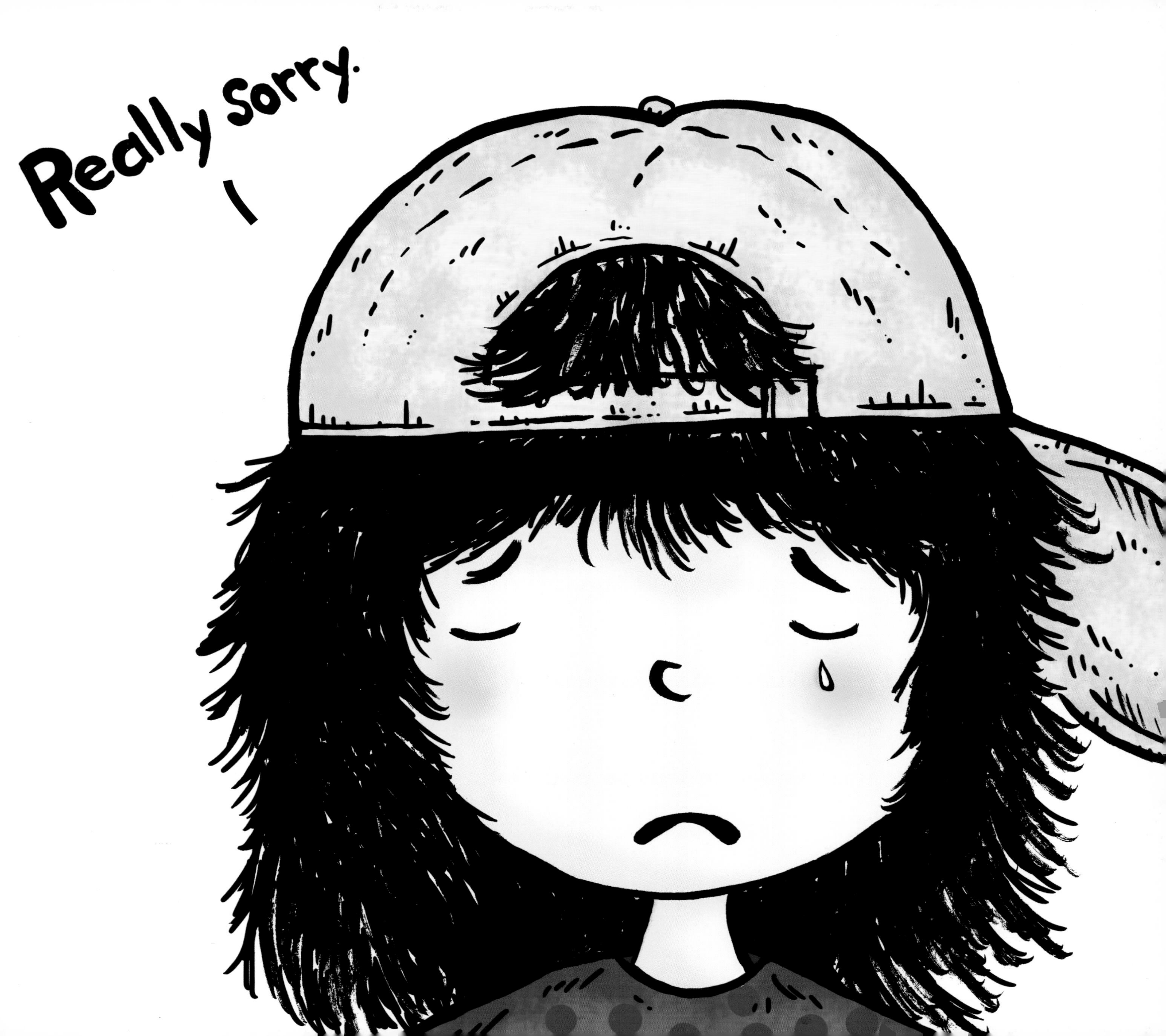
Really sorry.

9

DEAR MOM + DAD

B

F

A

Z

2

By the time you read this we'll be halfway to Outer Space in our Planetary Pirate Ship. (Home for dinner).

H

P

8

5